# Michelles Diary

## Sleepless nights

By Cathrine Mohambani

With thanks to my LORD and savior Jesus Christ, for the gift, love, and life he has given me. I hope to share this joy with young readers, I hope you love it. P.s this is not book one, if you want the release of book one comment and make a request.

# SLEEPLESS NIGHTS – diary of

## a brown haired girl

My sister and I had this tradition, we would watch a- movies at a on Friday afternoon, Saturday night, and on Sunday night. Sometimes on Saturday they would play cartoon movies or k¨ids movies — who doesn't love cartoons.

And on Sunday they loved playing scary movies. We loved watching them, even if it is extremely scary to the point of peeing your pans.

We did watch movies on other channels, but only if the movie playing in our channel is boring.

The reason we didn't tend to search other channels for movie night it is because we can watch that movie anytime during the week" when it plays again, and at a it repeats only once. Mom didn't like us watching scary movies. So, we would wait for her to doze off, on the couch and watch the movie. Ps we didn't have to wait that long.

I really didn't mind, even though I was a tiny bit scared or the fact that I didn't lik"e scary movies.

I wasn't worried because I had a plan. I shared a room and a bed with my sister Dineo, and if a scary monster would appear, crawling, creep or slivering under the bed, closet, window or door. I would k"ick" my sister off the bed, and that would

distract it for a while, I would
then mak"e a run for it.

ME KICKING DINEO OF THE BED

There is a Problem Tho with this Plan, Dineo got the corner side of the bed, it would be hard for me to k"ick" her off the bed.

I just hope she isn't having the same idea as mine, because that would be a Problem.

Sunday


Watching a movie on a school night is something that is very difficult to do. It's even worse when it is a scary movie.

Mom says watching scary movies is demonic and we might get possessed by it. She sometimes chases us back" to our room, and when she does, we would snick¨ back¨ to watch the movie.

DINEO AND I SNICKING OUT

The problem with that is we miss the introduction of the movie, which by the way is the important part of the movie because it draws you in.

BEING DROWN INTO THE MOVIE

That is how we would know if the movie is thrilling and worth our time; by the way, if we ever get caught snick"ing back" after being told to go to bed, all hell break"s loose.

ALL HELL BREAKING LOOSE

Monday

Today was a weird day at school. Teacher Vase or that's what we call him, was nowhere to be seen, which meant we had a free period. Unfortunately, I was stuck" with my super-annoying desk" mate, Valeria, who just wouldn't stop yapping about her week"end and favorite TV shows.

It was like she was on a mission to rub it in my face.

As if I didn't have enough problems, I asked her what channel they were on, and she told me "Channel 98.". Of course, we don't have that channel at home, and she knows that, and she just had to rub it in my face.

"I guess you don't have Premium channels," she said, with a smirk. She then continued blabbering on and on. I stopped listening and continued with

what I was good at; daydreaming.

I am not a very good judge of character; I regret that moment of desperation because I am suffering the consequences now.

Euv and I got separated last year, and we got placed in different classes because the teachers thought it would subside the chaos.

Euv made new friends and slowly forgot about me. Desperate situations call for desperate measures. I needed a friend ASAP—

more like I needed someone to make Euv jealous. Most of the fifth graders knew who I was.

ME TRYING TO MAKE FRINDS WITH MY CLASSMATES

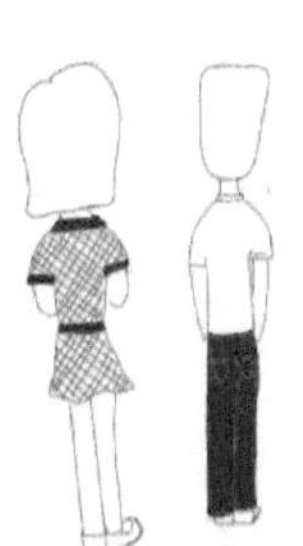

MY CLASSMATE NOT WANTING TO HANG OT WITH ME (I GUES I AM JUST TO COOL FOR THEM)

Valeria was the new k"id. As I said, desPerate times call for desPerate measures. Fast Forward, and I ended uP with her. Even after Euv and I made uP, she k"ePt on Following me.

Now I am Facing the Full Fire of my actions. IF I end uP in that situation again, I think" I would be better OFF with an imaginary Friend.

ME PLAYING HIDE AND SICK WITH MY
IMAGINARY FRIEND.

ME SAYING GOODBYE TO MY IMAGINARY
FRIEND BECAUSE I HAVE OUTGROWN IT.

When I got home from school, I
found Dineo on my side of the bed
and her book"s and bags on her
side.

If it were the other way around,
she would have thrown a fit.
When I say something, she would

say it is her room and that I am just a hobo who is just passing by. I didn't bother saying anything; what was on my mind was watching my shows before the world of channels consumed me.

I am staying faithful to my shows. I was glad today because I didn't have to fight with Dot for the remote or run crying because Mom changed the channel. I could watch in peace.

Tuesday


Today during break time, Valeria's friends came over to our table. They started talking about stuff like movies, shows, boys, and stuff.

I didn't know any of their shows and movies, and I wasn't that interested in them. I was kind of glad because I was able to easily zoom out of the conversation and continue writing.

I was writing my own play; I didn't use many words, but the illustrations were more like a comic book" than a manuscript.

I was in the zone when something
Pulled me to my senses but made
me lose my sanity when I heard the

voice of someone who caused the
light bulb in my brain burst and

who made my heart become a drummer.

It was Nathan. Oow! Roses are red, and violets are blue. Who needs the stars when you're starring in my fantasy? Who needs musicians when the sound of your voice is music to my ears?

How I wish in moments like this I was a poet instead of a storyteller because he makes me believe that I can fly.

While I was busy fantasizing about my whole life's adventure with him, I was given a platform to speak".

"Huh!" I answered the question he ask"ed that I did not hear.

"He ask"ed if you had seen the movie called The Goblin," said one of the girls. Before I could answer, Valeria interrupted.

"She probably hasn't. What is it like?" she ask"ed.

"It is so scary; I bet you girls won't be able to watch it," said Nathan's friend Gerald.

They then started talk"ing about scary movies.

"What about you? What scary movies have you watched?" ask"ed Nathan. I was then again put on stage. I told them about the scary movies Dineo and I have watched.

"Those are not that scary. There is a movie called Wrong Direction you should all watch; it is playing this Sunday night. I heard that it would be epic and horrifying. I heard it would give you nightmares for months. Let's see who is brave enough to watch it." Said Gerald.

"You're on," they agreed to watch it.

I was glad that our channel was not a Premium; I didn't have to watch it, and I wasn't planning on telling them. I wasn't in the mood to be chased by zombies or whatever in my dreams for months.

Being Chased by Zombies in my dream

I just stared, listened, and nodded.

"There is a problem, Tho; Michelle doesn't have a Premium channel." Said Valeria.

"No worries, it is playing on a Public channel." I had no choice but to agree.

After the conversation, a train of thoughts went in circles in my head.


I was think"ing about Nathan and the conversation we had, and I was also hoping that I didn't make a fool of myself.

Even though I wanted to focus on class, I kept trailing off. I had to stop so that I wouldn't get into trouble.

After class, I told Euv about it. I even asked him to join in. I told

him about the mom's issues with
horror films.

"I think" it would be a great idea
to watch it with you at your
place," I said.

He kept on giving excuses; he said it was not his turn to pick a movie this Sunday.

"I thought you only do that on Saturday."

"Yeah, well... well ahl We started doing it on Sundays too," he said.

I told him that he could make a deal with Peri, Euv's older brother.

"Plus, he loves horror. " He then told me that his mother doesn't allow him to watch TV on a school night. I didn't press any further.

Wednesday

My home is not far from school. Yesterday, I had a short amount of time to process the conversation I had with Nathan.

Today I plan to walk" back" home and allow the train of thoughts to go wild.

Today was sports day; we have it every Wednesday. The whole school is divided into teams.

We have the red team, the yellow team, the green team, and the blue team. And you have to wear the colour of your team. I got yellow, Euv got red, including Nathan. last year, when we found out that Euv and I got into different teams, Euv would come wearing a yellow T-shirt and join my team, and the following week" I would come wearing red and join his team. It was so much fun that we ended up doing the same with the other teams as well.

Until we got caught, because we became k"nown on every team, the teachers were confused.

"Hey, why are you wearing a blue t-shirt and not green?" said one teacher and the other would say,

"Why would they be on the blue team? They are on the red" and then it would go on and on.

It was a trivial matter; they didn't see the need to tell our parents; what they did was k̈eep an eye on us.

Now I was stuck" with Valeria on my team.

We were on the ground, literally sitting on the ground—this isn't one of those fancy schools where they have a mini—stadium for students to play all k"inds of sports. It was just a small open field, and we had to sit on the dusty ground where the grass was almost dried out. We were sitting there, watching our teams compete.

I am more of an indoor person than an outdoor sports girl. I don't k"now what they were think"ing

when they called me to the field
to race. Protesting didn't help
either.

had no choice but to race. There
were two students from each
team, and I didn't want to
disappoint my team. I was
think"ing, What if I was meant to
be an athlete? Maybe that is the
reason I never lik"ed it, because I

was meant to be one. What if it is the start of a new chapter? They were about to start the race, and I crouched down. I only needed to be in **1**st or **2**nd place; **3**rd is not an option.

"On your mark", get ready, set, go!" said the conductor. The moment the teacher said go, I was

very determined. I closed my eyes and ran as fast as I could, feeling the dusty air on my face and hearing the shouts of cheer from the other students.

This is the moment when everything changes, and that will be the start of my autobiography.


I wanted to peek" to see how close I was to the finish line. I opened my eyes with enthusiasm, to find that the other team had already crossed the finish line, and I was not even that far ahead of the starting line.

that is where my athletic dream
finished before it started. I
didn't even bother finishing the
race; I just went back" to my
seat.

My plan was to tak"e a walk" back"
home so that I could finish
processing the conversation I had
with Nathan, but first I had to
snick" away. When I was about to

leave, I found that my transport had already arrived, and the driver saw me, which meant I couldn't snick" away.

I was sitting on the table watching TV when my mom called.

She called lik"e a thousand times, and I didn't realize it until I felt

a smack" on the head and the TV
was turned off.

"Go and buy bread," said Mom.

"My show is about to start; I will
buy it when it's finished." I
protested.

"Go now." The look" she gave me
made me feel lik"e I was being
suck"ed into a black" hole.

I was leaving to go buy bread. I saw a small, bold round head peeping. It was that brat Peeping Tom who was at it again. How annoying he is.

"Why was your mother yelling at you?" He laughed. "Did she smack you again?"

"How is that any of your business?" I retorted.

"Were you sitting on top of the table again, watching TV?"

That brat is so annoying. If I had my way, I would tie him next to a rocket and program it to take him to whatever messed-up planet he creeped out of.

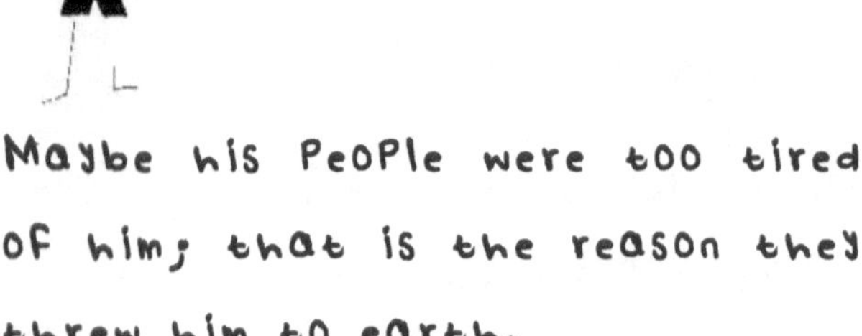

Maybe his people were too tired of him; that is the reason they threw him to earth.

Peeping Tom is my neighbour's kid who's really annoying and loves putting his nose into everyone's business.

There is a brick" fence that divides our house from his. He is always peeping and look"ing over here, which is creepy and annoying. He is the only child in his family, and it hasn't been long since his family moved into our neighbourhood. He always tries to start stupid conversations with us, and he loves mak"ing stupid jok"es.

Once, I was playing k"nock"out with the EUV and Tshepiso. Knock"out is a game where you must cross different obstacles without being k"nock"ed out.

At one of the obstacles, they
must get through me without
being k"nock"ed out.

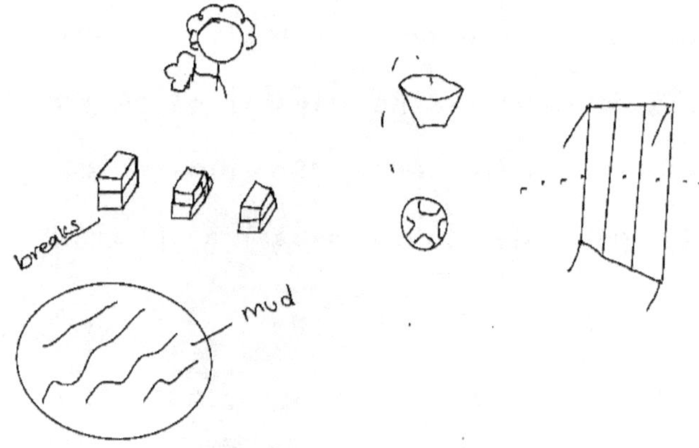


Peeping Tom wanted to join us,
so we let him because we needed
more players. His turn came, and
he went running through the layer
of brick"s.

On the side was a tub of dirty water. I pushed him, and he fell into the tub of water. We had to end the game there because he went home crying. I should have called him crying, baby Tom.

Thursday


I was still thinking of ways to sneak past Mom so I could be able to watch the movie wrong direction on Sunday night. I decided to call for reinforcement, Euv. When I got to Euv's place, he wasn't there; his mom said he went to play without me.

Since EUV and I got separated last year, he has made new friends, and I am slowly being forgotten. I don't see the need to have many friends; you can play with acquaintances. With lots of friends, you might end up financially embarrassed because you were unable to keep up with the birthday gifts you had to buy.

Plus, if you tell your secret to a large group of friends, there is a 100% chance that the whole world will find out. When I got back" home, Dineo and some of our friends were about to start a game.

Let me tell you, even though I was born African, that doesn't mean Africa was born in me.

I am horrible at playing traditional games lik"e wool, ball (which is called flori), sk"ipping rope [which is called k"azi], tighezo, and ice cream.

I am always Pick"ed last at these games, and I am only invited to Play when they are unevenly matched.

I am not much of a fan of either of these games, but if I want to look" cool in school, I have to be the best in these games and unmatched or unreplaceable, but one of the two is correct: I am unmatched.

I ask"ed them if I could join them. They all look"ed at each other.

"Sorry, but we already pick"ed our teams," said Ntsak"o. "Maybe the next game."

I waited and waited. I thought the next game would never come.

I saw that he was coming over; I think" his mom must have told him that I was look"ing for him. I was glad to see him. I went to him and dragged him to the game. He was against it at first, but he gave in after a round of bagging.

"This is my partner; we can now be even." They agreed; Euv is Indian, and I was hoping that he would mak"e me look" good.

Euv and I were on different teams.
We were playing ball.

One person would enter in the middle, and they have to stack bricks and push them to give their team member a life or an extra life, and they also have to avoid being hit by the other team members who are on both ends of the line.

If the person in the middle catches the ball while in the middle, they can throw it as far as they can.

I thought of this as an easy game. I was the only one left with a life from my team.

The moment I entered the middle,
I was going to mak"e history, and
everyone would remember my name.
It didn't tak"e more than five
seconds to be hit by the ball.

I wasn't worried; I thought Euv
must be far worse than me, booy!

I was wrong; he played lik"e a pro;
even though his moves were goofy,
he dogged the ball lik"e he was a
pro    player,    and    he    was
unteachable by our team.

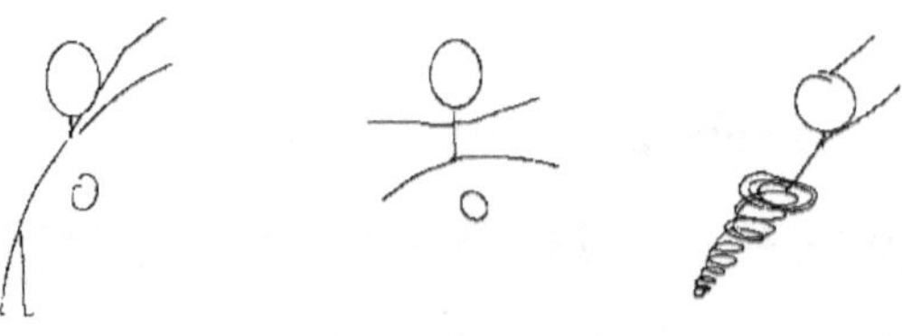

And as for me, my job was to
fetch the ball each time the
other team threw it.


And I think" I might have gotten
a concoction from the last blow
to the head.

I was losing interest in the game because I was tired of being the ball girl.

Friday


Euv came to my class today; I guess he remembered that he had a best friend. "Hey M. We are going to catch some snack's. Want to come?"

I thought maybe the sun was shining in the wrong part of his brain, and that is the reason his vocabulary is verbing.

"Come on," he persisted when I didn't give a response. Can you blame me?

He took¨ my hand and dragged me behind the girls' and boys' bathrooms.

I ask¨ed what we were doing there.

"We're here to catch some snack"s." I look"ed at him, waiting for an explanation. He pointed at a group of students who were crouching down and putting stick"s inside a hole. I look"ed closer, and it look"ed lik"e they were catching...

"Termites? Are they catching termites"? I ask"ed Euv.

"Yes, that is our snack"." I shook" my head in response. He pleaded, but I continued to refuse. I turned and was about to leave when I heard

"Nathen," someone I don't k"now was calling his name.

You should have seen me; I span and turned lik"e Hurricane Katrin. When I look"ed, he was standing there, hanging with his friends.

"Ok"ay, let's go catch some snack"s," she said, a little enthusiastic. I grabbed him, and we went to the termite hole. I am a Pro at catching termites, even though I don't eat them. I tried it once; they are crunchy and testy, but my eyes betrayed my stomach.

There is a place back" home where we used to catch termites with Peri; he was the one who introduced us to them, but now they look" lik"e wild ants and are not meant for eating. Euv gave me his container where I can put them.

Euv k"nows that when he catches the termite with me, he will get a lot because I don't lik"e them. I was ready to show off my sk"ills to Nathan. I was all over the place, trying to impress him. My eyes were on and off him. I felt a burning sensation on my neck"; it was becoming more and more painful. That's when I realized

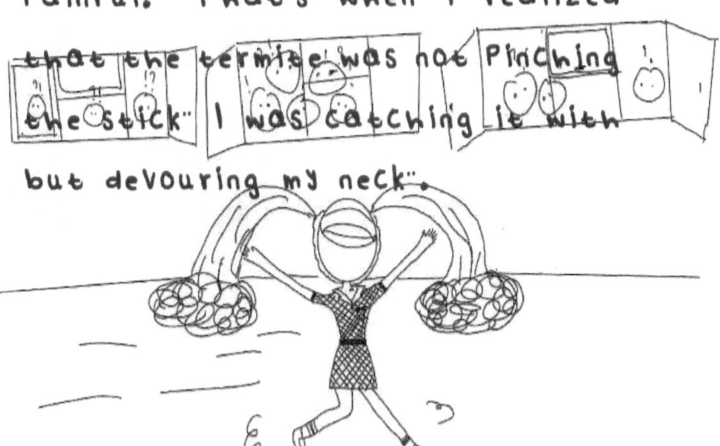

that the termite was not pinching the stick" I was catching it with but devouring my neck".

The moment I realized that I went flying like a lunatic trying to remove the termite from my neck", and when I realized that it was gone, I calmed down and evaluated the situation. I then turned to see a dozen eyes from a portion of the school on me.




Some other students were peck"ing through the windows, some came out of the toilets, and the rest just followed the noise.

I bet that they now think" I am crazy. I was somewhat nol extremely embarrassed that I didn't even check" to see if Nathan saw that.

I Put my head high, laughed slightly, Pretended that nothing had happened, and then left the Premises.

I hid from everyone, especially Nathan, and waited for the bell to ring. I wished the sk"y would Just open and swallow me.

I wish it had happened on the last day of school; I wouldn't have to show my face for a while, and when school reopened, everyone would have already forgotten the drama.


Saturday


Sometimes we get really excited about things, and we forget to think" about what could go wrong. We Just think" about all the fun stuff, you k"now?

Week"ends I k"now it is a time when you sleeP in because, during the week", you have to wak"e uP early for school. It is different for me; if I don't wak"e uP early on a Saturday, there won't be a difference between week"ends and week"days. If I wak"e uP late, I won't get the chance to watch TV until late in the afternoon because the PeoPle here love hogging the remote. I wok"e uP early in the morning and snuck" to watch TV. The silence was so refreshing.

In the afternoon, I was lying on the floor watching TV.

Dot was doing her own stupid things while Mom was cooking in the kitchen. Our house is not that big, so you can see the kitchen, and you can even watch TV while in the kitchen. Dineo said it out of the blue to Mom.

"I want to have my own room; I am
tired of sleeping with Michelle."

She then pulled out an imaginary
list of things she was tired of.
She said she was also tired of
sharing a bed with me. She's the
one to talk. She is an actual pig.

It would be nice to have my own space, my own room, and a double bed all to myself. I can already see it—fresh air, a tidy room,

Posters of strangers not on the wall. Silence, total silence. (Freedom is coming tomorrow.)

Dineo and I are like Tom and Jerry.

There is always an uproar between us. I remember a few week"s ago, Euv and I decided to do a prank" week".

I learned some of the prank"s from watching Mr. Bone. I was in our room, and I called her to come over for a moment. When she arrived, I slammed the door on her face. How is it my fault that she lack"s humour? She went crying to Mom.

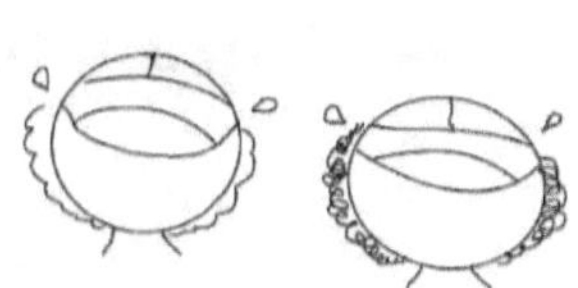

EUV has a rubber snak"e; we
threw it on her while she was
eating, and she ended up spilling
a bowl of cornflak"es on Dot.


Euv and I got punished that day.
We even tried the prank" where
you put the buck"et filled with

water on top of the door, that one was an epic failure because, between Euv and me, I am a little bit taller than him; in other words, we couldn't reach the door, plus the buck"et of water was too heavy for us to carry.

We had put a rain check" on that prank". I can't help it if she's a scary cat, and don't say that I am the reason she wants her own room.

The room is always upside down, and when it's her turn to mak"e the bed, she only tidies her side. She is always on the phone when

I am trying to do my homework"; she even wears my clothes without my authorization and hogs the blank"et. I think" I am the one who is suffering. I didn't think" she was serious because she always said she wanted her own room, but when it came nighttime, she changed her mind.

That made everyone in the house not tak"e her seriously, but I do want my own room too. I also decided to pitch in and convince Mom that we should have our own rooms. Mom agreed, and then I started to move out.

I remember when we first moved here; it was a long time ago, and back" then I was still sharing a room with Dineo.

When we arrived, I was still admiring the new house; I didn't realize that Dineo had already left.

When I entered the house, I was too late; she had already called dibs on the second-biggest room.

I went to the first-biggest room and called Dibs.

"That is mom and my small dad's room, stupid."

I ended up with the smallest of the three rooms. It was more like a closet than a room. A small room needs a small bed.

I hate clatter; it mak"es me feel suffocated.

The room is small but cosy. I ended up spending the rest of my day cleaning and pack"ing.


Sunday

Today I was excited to move into my new room. When we were at church, I k"ept think"ing about my room.

Even in Sunday school, the teacher applauded me for being quiet and attentive; she didn't k"now I was lost in thought.

I was glad she didn't ask me any questions; if she did, she would have known that I wasn't listening.

She only asked those who were making noise. The only thing that could pull me out of my train of thought was the music.

After church, Dineo finished decorating her room. I am not skilled in decorating or interior design, so my room was plain and simple, or, in other words, boring.

At least I don't have to wake up
to pictures of strangers staring
at me—creepy; very creepy.

When it was evening and close to
movie night, we were all sitting in
the sitting room, watching TV,
except for Dot, who was asleep on
the sofa, and Dad, who went out.

"Michelle, come scratch my head;
it's itchy," called out Mom. She

says that when she is tired, she wants her head massaged.

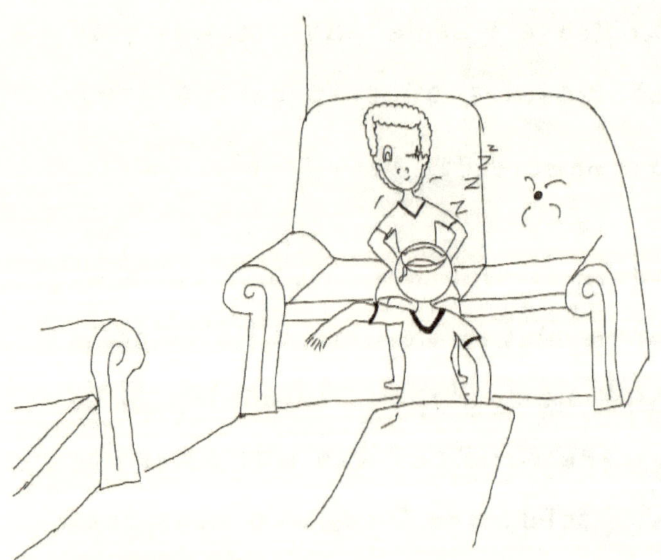

The moment I touched her head, she fell asleep instantly.

If she only k"new that the way to get her head massaged every day was to allow us to watch TV on a school night, she would be the happiest woman in the world.

 I told Dineo to put on the movie called Wrong Direction that Gerald was talk"ing about on channel 81. The movie was about to start, and Mom tried to wak"e up.

I continued to scratch her head, and she fell asleep again. I wasn't about to miss the introduction. Just by the introduction, you can tell that this movie will be brutal.

The sound was so loud that it made me jump to my seat. I quick"ly told Dineo to reduce the volume because Mom might wak"e up and tell us to go to sleep. I was shak"ing in my seat. It was lik"e I could feel the presence of the zombies in the room. What was missing were thunder and lightning. If Mom wasn't sleeping in the sitting room, I would have screamed my lungs out.

What I got from today is that when I don't want to get into trouble, the trick" is to do what

I do best—daydream. It also helps

in avoiding answering questions.
The second thing is a way to
watch movies on a school night,
and the third is that I now k"now
what they mean when they say
horror films.

Monday

When I wok"e up this morning, I
found myself in my new room. I
guess I dozed off while watching
the movie, and Dad must have
carried me to my room.

I guess Dad got the memo.

I can't believe I slept in my own
room for the first time alone, and
I didn't even realize it. I thought
it would be hard or that I would
be crying over Dineo. The movie
was scary though and I couldn't
get it out of my mind.

I was a little paranoid; my house
is loud, and when it is quiet, even
for a little bit, I feel like the

Zombies have invaded the territory.

I watched the movie, which shows that I am not a scary cat but strong and brave. I hope Nathan likes strong women.

I was a bit eager for the first break" to start so that we could talk" about the movie. When it was break" time, I waited and listened to others' conversations. I was prepared. Nobody was bringing up the topic of the movie, not even Velaria and her friend; they weren't even in class for half the break" time, even though they went to Nathan's class to chat without me. I was in on the agreement, wasn't I? I decided to go peek" at his class. Their class is next to ours; my class is in the middle, and on my right is Euv's class. I passed by the window a couple of times to see if I could spot Nathan or Valaria.

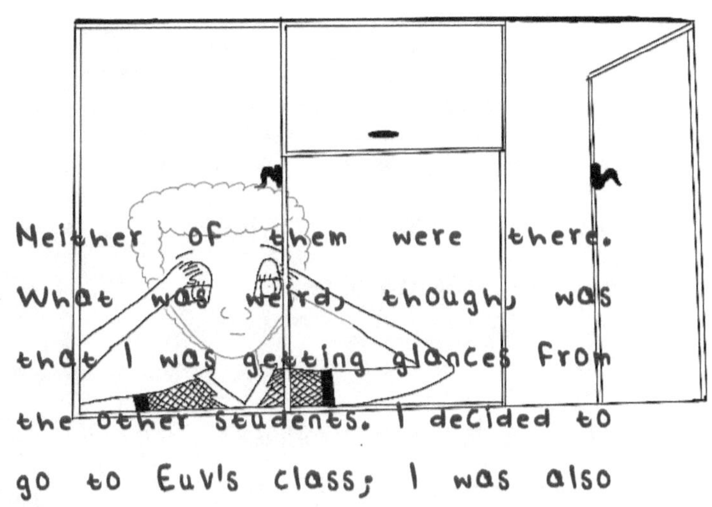

Neither of them were there. What was weird, though, was that I was getting glances from the other students. I decided to go to Euv's class; I was also getting glances, and everyone was whispering. Some boys in Euv's class started screaming and yelling like a maniac. I told EUV about this, and he looked like he knew the reason. I forgot the show I put on on Friday. I thought the weekend was enough for everyone to forget about the incident; I guess they did not have enough time to laugh or talk about it on Friday. I understand that it was funny, but I also don't get why the other students are mad at me, I told him.

He told me to follow him, and he led me behind the boy's and girl's bathrooms.

Apparently, they had put poison in the termites to exterminate them because of what happened on friday. Some of the students found my act funny, and others hated me because I was the reason there would no longer be free snack"s.

When I went back to class, Valeria was with her friends at our table. They scattered when I arrived.

"How is your neck?" she asked while snickering. I ended up spending my Monday filled with mockery, glances, and whispers.

When it was time for bed, I went to Dineo's room, and she closed the door on my face. I forgot I have my own room now. I read my Bible and prayed.

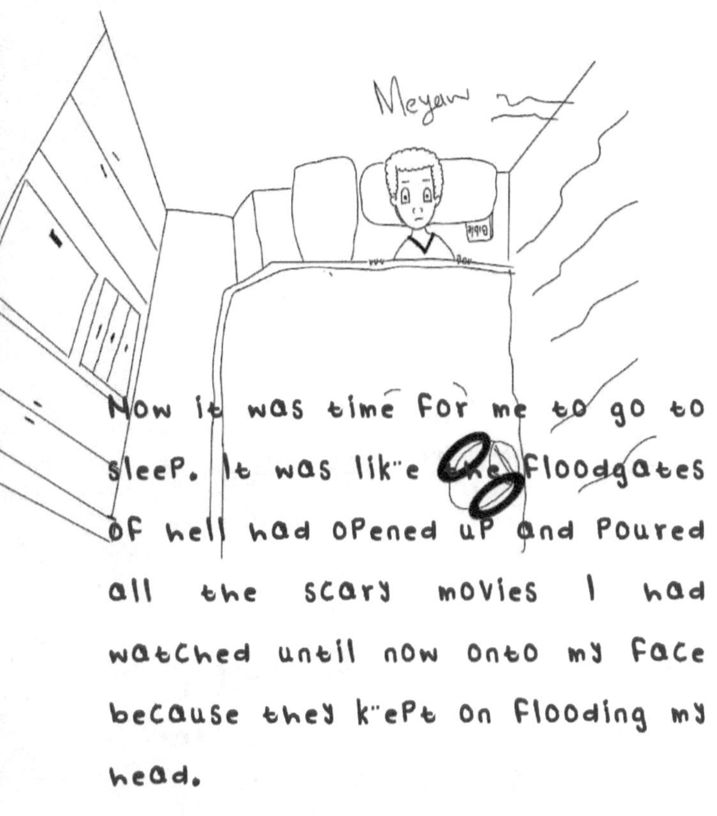



Now it was time for me to go to sleep. It was like the floodgates of hell had opened up and poured all the scary movies I had watched until now onto my face because they kept on flooding my head.

It felt like something was breathing on my neck" right next to me. I could hear all k"inds of crazy sounds.

If something creeps, crosses, or sliders in, I don't have a bargaining chip, so no Dineo to k"ick" off the bed. I then heard something squeaking.

I screamed out of the room and banged on Dineo's door.

She told me to get lost. I thought of sitting right at the door until she opened up, but the hallway was dark" and cold, just like" in the movie.

I decided to calm down and think" of a solution. I couldn't go to my room and shut my eyes. What if the zombies attack"ed while I was asleep?

I decided to k"eep watch. I went to the k"itchen, turned on the lights, and took a pan.

I then went to the seating room and turned on the TV and lights.

What calms me down and mak"es me feel better are cartoons. I Put on cartoons. I don't k"now what's wrong with this world.

I felt lik"e I was being mock"ed because the cartoons that were Playing were scary ones—not that scary in the daytime, but it felt scary right now. I decided to Put on cartoons Dot watches the baby ones. Her annoying, cringe cartoons didn't feel cringe at that moment.


Tuesday


I have gotten into trouble today because I kept dozing off in class. Can you blame me? I couldn't close my eyes, not even for a little bit, because either I felt something screeching, crying, breathing, or peeping, waiting for me to doze off, and every time I did, I had nightmares. When it started being bright outside, I went back" to my room so that nobody could find out that I hadn't slept the whole night.

The good thing about being tired is that I couldn't hear Valeria blabbering. The students were still laughing and whispering behind my back, it didn't help that I was punished by the teacher for dozing off during class. She made me stand in front of the whole class for the whole class to make fun of the class clown,

and the other teacher punished
me by mak"ing me clean the whole
class by myself after school. Euv
stayed behind and helped me with
the cleaning; even though he was
mak"ing a mess, I was too tired to
care.


The transport had already left
when we finished cleaning the
class, so we had no choice but to
walk" home. When Euv and I tak"e

a walk" together, we end up always tak"ing forever to reach our destination.

We carried each other on piggyback"; we tried froggy jumping our way back" and doing a back" flip to see who could reach the farthest.

We quit halfway through becaus Euv and I are k"ind of competitive and lazy in some areas. walk"ing back" home doesn't need to be boring.

Wednesday

I am kind of getting a little bit better. I was able to snooze off for a couple of minutes without a nightmare. I was dreaming about Dot's annoying, cringey cartoons.

I was bored today. I lay on the sofa, head facing down.

I already finished my shows, and what was playing on the other channels I watched, I had already seen. I kept scrolling through the channels, hoping to discover a whole new world.

I guess that my constant changing of channels must have annoyed Mom because the next thing she took" the remote from me and put in a different show. I just left and went outside, look"ing for something to do.

While I was leaving, I saw Peeping
Tom Peeping.

were always Playing in our streets;
I went to them and ask"ed them
to Play with them.

"We don't have enough Players," they said.

I waited a little bit. I saw Euv and his buddies, deciding to run to him, but the girls got to them before I could. They invited him and his buddy to Play with them. Hey, guess what? I was mismatched again. I had no one to Pair with because no one wanted me on their team. Euv wanted to quit and let me Play. I told him that he didn't have to, because if he did, I wouldn't Play either, and if I didn't, they wouldn't Play because they didn't have enough Players. I left there. I want to admit that I am also bummed out.

I ended uP Playing wool with Dot
and PeePing Tom at home at the
back" because I look"ed Pathetic.
Hey, I had to Practice; one day
they will want me on their team.


Thursday

Slowly but surely, the nightmares were beginning to be history, but still, I had no leverage, no one to distract the monster with as I made a run for it.

Dot was still sleeping with Mom and Dad. I had an idea to convince Mom and Dad to allow Dot to share a room with me, and when I became a master at swordsmanship and fighting and declared myself ready to face the monsters, I could tell the hobo to move out of my room.

That is a great Plan, but First
I had to convince my Parents. I
didn't want to tell them directly;
they might catch on. I told them
that it is a great idea to teach
children independence at a young
age, that Dot is old enough to
Fly on her own, and that if they
keep on babying her, she won't
grow up. Mom caught my drift on
what I was trying to say and
allowed Dot to share a room with
one of us. The Plan back-fired on

me; she didn't want to share a room with me but Dineo.

I was surprised that Dineo agreed to share a room with her when it was her idea to have her own room.

She and Dot are always skimming together; this is a downside of being a middle child.

Mom found out about me dozing off in class and that I sleep late every night watching cartoons.

I got a shouting, a scolding; for Africans, there is no grounding; it is either your hand, a shoe, a belt, or anything else that is around that can act as a weapon. I didn't get a smack" because she got a chance to cool down before I got home. I was grateful to the Lord for that. The person who spilt the beans was Mum Gobos Nyik"o, who can k"eep her mouth shut. She is the newspaper of the neighbourhood.    I    guess    her ambition is to become the biggest liar in town. I guess she takes it from her mom, who only comes to your place if she has news or is looking for news. I think she has superpowers. How can you explain her always knowing what new things you have brought? I think Peeping Tom is looking better compared to her.

Now I couldn't sneak out to watch TV because now mom's seances were activated. Now I had to find ways to survive the night. I couldn't sleep with the lights turned off. I turned the lights on and created my own imaginary place with family and friends;

they all lived in a big, beautiful house full of life, colours, and light. I started creating a story and an adventure for my characters. The main character was a boy named Nick". He didn't have a mom and a dad, but he lived with his adopted family, who loved him so much. Being in my imaginary world distracted me from other things. I was able to doze off for a while, and each time I wok"e up in the middle of the night, I would find someone had turned off the lights. I would wak"e up, turn the lights on, go back" to my imaginary world, and then doze off to sleep again.

Friday

I keep on saying this, but I'm serious; I am getting better. I realized that I shouldn't think about scary things or movies, and that really helps.

Well, when the world is against you, it will nibble your bottom.

In class today, I guess everyone forgot about the show I performed last Friday because they had started a new topic. When I came to class, Valeria and her group were chatting. When I listened closer, they were talking about the scary movie that played on Sunday. I wasn't that thrilled about the conversation. I was glad that they weren't sitting at our table.

"Hey, Nathan Gerald. Have you seen the movie?" asked one of the girls.

I looked behind me, and there he was.

I was shak"ing all over, and my heart was Pounding Fast. When he is around, I can't think" straight.

He approached them, and I was about to leave when he invited me closer with his sweet, sweet smooth talk".

"Aren't you going to Join us?" He ask"ed, and I nodded.

I regretted it when they continued talk"ing about the movie. I had to think" deeper into the horrible memories that I have buried.

"Hey, there will be a sequel to the movie on Sunday," said Gerald, and everyone agreed to watch. I don't k"now how I was dragged into this situation.

Saturday

Since the morning, there had been low shedding, Plus it was hot outside, lik"e **1000** degrees. It was hard to sleep, Plus, how can you sleep with vampire mosquitoes hovering around?

Who needs an alarm clock" that you barely hear when you have a Personal Flying machine in your own room that also k"eePs you active? Maybe I should think" of beComing a sales agent? and who needs mosquitoes when you have a mother who is against your Peaceful sleeP? She wok"e me uP, saying she was doing laundry and I needed to unfold my clothes, Plus that I was stink"ing uP the room.

It was so hot that no kid was playing in the street, and you could see the ghosts of the neighbourhood {people you never see outside}. I was kind of glad that Mom was doing laundry that day, even though I had to pitch in.

We might not have fancy pools like other places, but we do have tubs. I was also glad that we don't have washing machines and do our laundry by hand. When mom was done with laundering, I told her I would empty the tub.

She then left and went to Euv's place to talk to his mom. When they start talking, don't ever look forward to the end of the conversation. You can go to Joburg and back, and they will still be talking.

I dipped myself in the tub with my clothes still on, and it was so refreshing.

I could see the steam coming out. Dot joined in, even though Dineo, no matter how she think"s she is an adult, can't resist the fact that it is too hot to act cool. Peeping Tom was Peeping, and I acted lik"e I couldn't see him.

Euv Also came over, and we started splashing each other with water. Some kids from our neighbourhood saw us, and they came over.

They brought with them water guns, and others brought water balloons. We started shooting each other with the water gun and chasing one another with water balloons. I felt sorry for Peeping Tom, so I ended up inviting him. We then started chasing each other with buckets of water splashing on each other. When everyone left, it was a mess, and I had to clean it up because Mom was so mad. When I was done cleaning up, I was all dried up. That is how hot it was.

Sunday

I was so anxious because the scary movie was playing today. I don't k"now what happened in church because I barely listened, but I listened today when the pastor preached.

I was worried and think"ing a lot about the movie. I was pulled out of my thoughts when the pasta said this.

"Do not fear." That caught my attention. "Do not fear, for I am with you; don't be afraid, for I am your God."

He talk"ed about God not giving
us a spirit of fear but of love,
power, and a sound mind. That
the Lord is look"ing after us and
not to be afraid of the enemy.

I thought about what he said, and he was right. I shouldn't be afraid it is just a movie, and what they are playing in the movie is not real. I got this.

When it was time for movie night. I was sitting on the long sofa so that I could lie down when watching the movie.

Dineo was on the other long sofa with her blank"et. We didn't need to scratch or massage Mom's head because she left to go to sleep before the movie could start. I didn't want her to go, but it was out of my hands.

The movie was about to start, and my heart was beating like crazy. I made a silent prayer and told Jesus that I was afraid, and I was sorry because You said not to be afraid.

scared of having nightmares or sleeping alone.

I don't k"now what got into me, but I couldn't stop Pleading with God. I guess I am not as brave as I thought. Mom then wok"e uP From her slumber, and you could hear her FootstePs—our house is not that big. She then turned the TV oFF without a word and told us to go to sleeP. The intro to the movie hadn't even started. I was hoping he would tak"e my Fear of watching the movie away, but this could work".

When I was in my room, getting ready for sleep, I told Him that He was with me and protecting me from the creepy crawly and the slithering. If it's true, I ask"ed Him to tak"e my fear of sleeping alone away and let me have sweet dreams.


Monday

I slept like a baby. I couldn't believe that my prayer was heard. I cried because it had been days since I had a good night's rest. I was grateful to God.

It was a holy day today, which meant no school. I was so happy that I slept well. I decided to watch all my favourite shows. In life, you will face big boulders, and mine is Dineo.

I fought with her for the remote.

When I stood up for a second, just a second to go and help myself or take a little break", when I came back", I would find that she had changed the channel.

I planned to do the same, so I waited for her to leave. It is impossible to sit the whole day and not use the bathroom. She finally stood, and when I was about to change the channel, I found out that she had taken the remote and hid it. Dineo has been hiding things from me for like forever, so I knew most of her hiding places, and I was able to find the remote where she hid it.

She hid it inside the serial box.
{maybe I should become a detective}

I changed the channel. When she came back", she was so mad that she pounced on me, and we ended up fighting.

Mom was right about being possessed; maybe she is possessed.

I had to let her win because mom told me to go buy bread. You might ask" why I am always the one who is being sent to buy bread; well, I am the better option. When Dineo is sent to buy bread, the bread would arrive, but without the change, and if she sends Dot 'her baby', she would whine first and then goes to the mark"et and back" without the bread, or she would bring the wrong thing because she forgot what she was supposed to buy.

Then again, they might be doing this on purpose so they can't be sent to the mark"et; those two are always scheming.

I met with Euv. On my way to the store, He told me that there was a baby k"itten left in Troy's place.

I went to check" it out; they were so cute. I wish I had a Pet, but I first have to get my own Place before that could happen. We later met with his friends on the way to the store; we Played a little game of tag, and after that, they had a debate about stupid things.

I couldn't tell them that to their faces because Euv was also involved in the stupid debate. I had to back" him up because he's my best friend. It's a must to have each other's back".

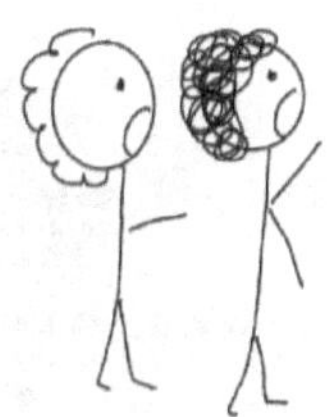

I had to tak"e his side and fend for him, but if it was him and me having a debate about stupid things, there was no friendship involved.

I told Euv about the scary movie, sleeping alone, and the prayer I made. I thought he would laugh at me, but he told me, if I am scared of them, why do I watch them? I later realized he wasn't that macho about scary movies either. It was a little bit dark" when I arrived home with the bread. As I said, I am still standing by what I said; I am the better option most of the time.


Tuesday


When it was break" time, everybody went out for lunch, and

I stayed behind. Shaun and Max also stayed behind. We talk"ed about the show Samurai, which he is also a Fan OF. We started role-Playing, and I showed OFF my samurai moves.

We had to stop mid-way because the other students started coming back".

Valeria called me over and we stood with her friends outside our classroom.

I was hoping that they wouldn't talk" about the movie; it is not that I am scared, but also because I didn't watch the movie. I didn't want to be laughed at, especially by Nathan.

I tried my best today to avoid talk"ing about the movie.

When they started wanting to start the topic of the movie, I told them I had to finish my activity. I think" I have become paranoid because I thought Valeria wanted to talk" about the movie, so I pretended to be sleeping.

When I got home, I was exhausted.


Wednesday

Today on the sports field, we weren't forced to do any sports; they even left us to mix with the

Other team because they were focused on training those who were 'athletic' according to them because they would soon be competing with other Primary schools.

Valeria dragged me to her friends.

I don't k"now why she lik"es dragging me into her business; I think" it is a habit.

I could see the determination on her face. I found out too late that she was desperate because she wanted to discuss the movie.

I want to say it is because she was really intrigued by the movie and wanted to share her enjoyment with us. {If I didn't spend a year with her due to circumstances, I would say that} but I k"now she wants to show that she saw the movie.

That is brutal, and she is brave.
I had no choice but to tell them
that I didn't watch the movie,
and they made fun of me.

"What is so funny?" Asked
Gerald.

They told him that I'd chicken
out. "I guess the movie was too
scary for her".

"Don't worry, I didn't watch it
either." I raised my head to see
who it was, and I realized that
it was Nathan.

He told me that he's not a big fan of scary movies lik"e Gerald and the Girls. He also told me something weird: if you don't lik"e something or are scared of something, you shouldn't force yourself to watch it or do it.

It was like what Euv said the other day. We then continue talking about our favourite shows and why we dislike horror films.

He said he only watched scary movies because he saw that others were doing the same, and I told him the same thing. Just by doing that, I had the best day ever.

I ended up snicking away from our transport driver because I needed to digest everything Nathan and I talked about.

I took" another route back" home so he would see me. Mom didn't lik"e me walk"ing back" home because apparently, I was wasting transport money. Dad, on the other hand, encourages it; he says it is good to exercise instead of watching TV the whole day. When I wanted to avoid scolding,

I told Dad that I felt like exercising because I had been sitting and watching TV a lot, and he would take my side in the war that was about to erupt.

Thursday

I slept with the light off. I was happy about that, even though when I went to sleep the lights were on. I guess Mom turned them off or Dad; I don't think it was Dad because when he is asleep, he is asleep, like a rock. Anyway, I didn't wake up to turn on the light; I just left my door open so

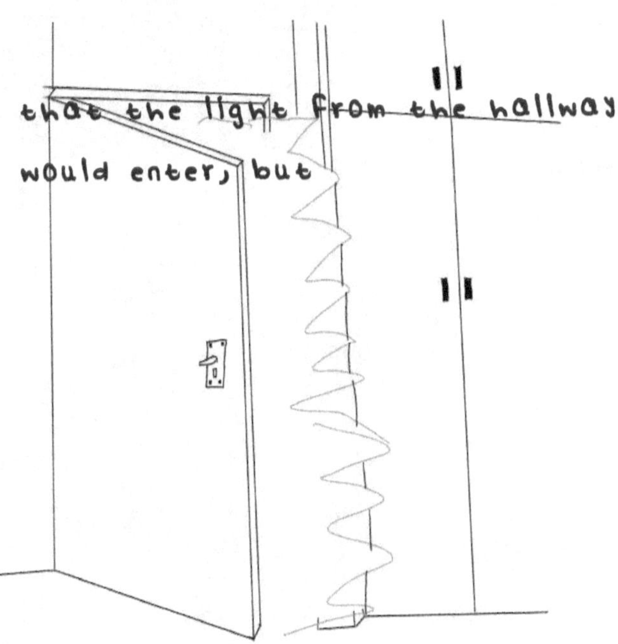


I did hide my head under my
blank"et and remind myself that I
am not alone; God is with me.

Then I thought about my
imaginary world.

After school today, I saw Dad and
Mom.

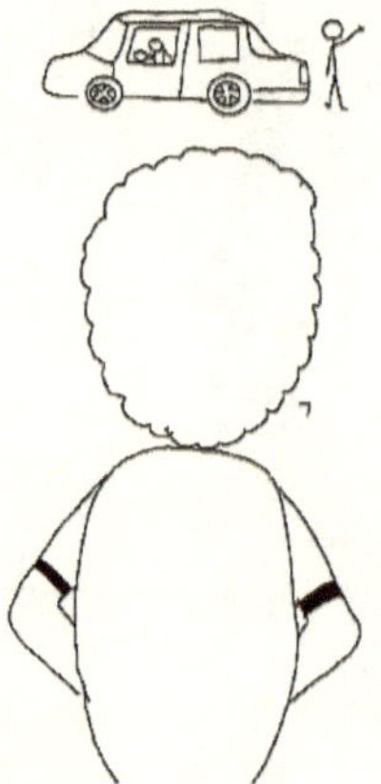

I thought they were coming to
pick" us up.

I didn't think" I got into that
much trouble because our school
calls parents in, if the k"id has
done something seriously good or
bad, and I don't think" I did
neither, maybe bad but what I

did isn't that terrible to call my parents. I just fell in the middle, or maybe I did something really bad without knowing. I approached the car really slowly, with caution.

Dot came running to hug Dad. He then led her to the car and gave me a bag with a change of clothes. I was confused. He told me that we would be walking home.

I then retreated from everything. Taking a 'walk' with Dad is torture.

I wanted Mom to save me; she just started the car and left with Dot.

We took" a walk", and drop by at my grandParents' Place to greet them which is really Far From my Place, but not that Far From school, it is like when you race you take ten twenty steps back" From the starting" line. We then took" the long road back" home.

On the good side of walk"ing with Dad, he got me ice cream on our way back".

I was told to tak"e a bath the moment I arrived home. Less TV time.

Friday

Dad also fetched me and Dot today. We had to walk" back" home; I don't k"now what's need of torturing me. I was glad Euv agreed to walk" back" home with us. I walk"ed so slowly with Euv that Dad and Dot were far ahead; that they look"ed lik"e peanuts.

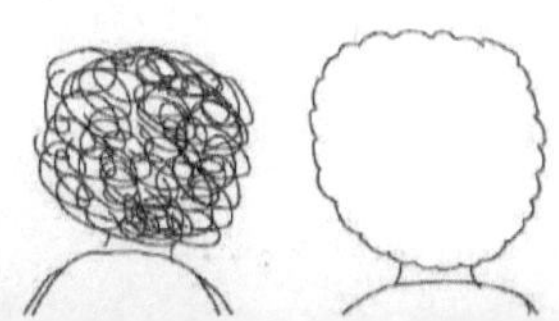

Dad was carrying Dot on his back". I wish it was me. We took" another road and visited my grandParent's Place with Euv.

Grandma ask"ed why I didn't come with Dad today. I told my grandma that Dad was carrying heavy stuff, and that was the reason he wasn't able to come. Friday's show was about to begin. And I wasn't going to miss it because of a crazy walk".

Grandma made us something to eat while we were watching TV with Grandpa. After he invited us to play chess with him, he loved it very much, and when we came over, he always wanted to play with us.

"Do you remember what I taught you?" He ask¨ed me "You should be a pro by now".

I told him that I don't get much practice. Plus, it is more fun to play with others.

I played five games, and he beat me at all five. I then played with Euv to console myself. I beat him. We didn't even realize how late it was, and they were look"ing for us back" home.

I k"new I was in big trouble, so I ask"ed GrandPa to let us stay the night. Even the whole year, if possible.

They agreed, and even Euv's mom agreed. My grandParents' house is big, so it is fun staying there. We ran around chasing each other; we even Played Samaria, annoying my aunt.
Later that night, we watched war movies with GrandPa.

Euv and I slept late last night.
We had no one to tell us to go
to sleep, and because the house
was too big, anyone could hardly
hear us.
We played truth or dare and
dared each other to go to
different parts of the house alone
in the dark".

We even made ghost sounds. Aunty
T ended up wak"ing up and
dragging us to sleep while Pulling
us with our ears. Ouch!


Saturday


In the morning, Dad came by and
brought me clothes to change
into. He also came to Pick" up Euv.
I was saddened, but not ready to
leave. He didn't look" mad; that is

the k"ind of person he is: chilled.
I didn't want to k"now how Mom
was doing. He ask"ed me when he
should pick" me up. I told him
tomorrow.

I was fed, washed, and spoiled. I
played chess with Grandpa and he
told wise tales.

I should come more often.

When night arrived, I watched a movie with Auntie T because Grandpa was too tired to watch, and Grandma was not a TV person.

The dreaded time arrived. I had forgotten that I was a coward for sleeping alone, plus this house was big, and anyone would barely hear me when I screamed.

I prayed and lay on the bed.

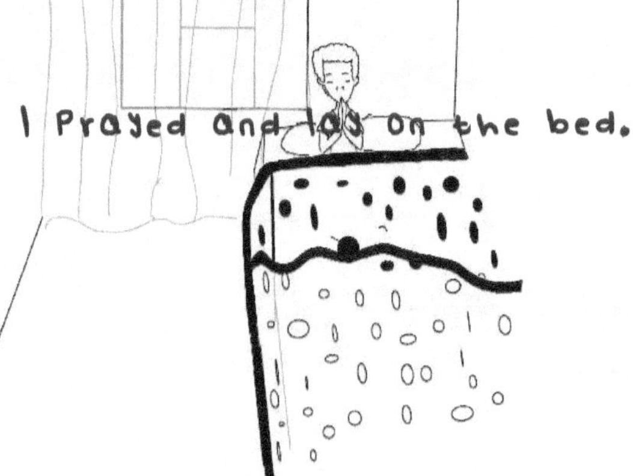